Perhaps Champlain is not one of the "great lakes." It is certainly a good lake—and—at least in my estimation, one of the countries "better" lakes.

It is about 120 miles long, plunging like a dagger from Quebec and filleting Vermont from New York State. It's about 11 miles wide at its widest.

And the ever-changing surface of Lake Champlain is like a screen that conceals Vermont's oldest and most enduring mystery.

Oddly, Lake Champlain is on approximately the same latitude as the infamous "Loch Ness." That, in part, may explain why hundreds of people claim to have encountered "something mysterious" in the lake.

And that "something"—whatever it may be—is apparently alive.

Also by Joseph A. Citro

Fiction

*Shadow Child**
*Guardian Angels**
*Lake Monsters**
*The Gore**
*Deus-X: The Reality Conspiracy**
*Not Yet Dead**

Books That Might Not Be Fiction

Green Mountain Ghosts, Ghouls, and Unsolved Mysteries
Passing Strange—True Tales of New England Hauntings and Horrors
Green Mountains, Dark Tales
Cursed in New England: Stories of Damned Yankees
Curious New England: The Unconventional Traveler's Guide to Eccentric Destinations
Weird New England
The Vermont Ghost Guide
The Vermont Monster Guide
*Joe Citro's Vermont Odditorium—Strange Tales of Vermont and Vermonters**
*Vermont's Haunts—Tall Tales and True from the Green Mountain State**

(*indicates titles available from Crossroad Press)

Design by Aaron Rosenberg

ISBN 978-1-937530-60-0

 For information address Crossroad Press at 141 Brayden Dr., Hertford, NC 27944

www.crossroadpress.com

Joe Citro's Vermont Odditorium

Strange Tales
of Vermont & Vermonters

Joseph A. Citro

CONTENTS

1. What Lies Beneath Lake Champlain?
2. Danville's Divine Comedy
3. Cow Kill—A Shocking Tale
4. UVM's Tenured Terrors
5. The Bennington Triangle
6. Emily's Bridge
7. Windsor's Water Sprite
8. Those Enigmatic Eddys

INTRODUCTION

Here are eight of my favorite stories.

When I began researching and writing about Vermont weirdness, circa 1990, these were among the first tales that seized my attention. I think of them as classic tales of the state's high strangeness: Champ, the Eddy Brothers, the Bennington Triangle, Emily's haunted covered bridge... the list goes on.

I had been telling such tales on Vermont Public Radio since 1992. My first book-length collection came out in 1994. So it was only a matter of time until the idea of an audiobook came up. I don't even remember whose idea it was. I suspect the suggestion was made by any number of people who attended my readings or lectures. Or maybe the idea came from my friend Chris Albertine, the brilliant audio engineer who recorded most of my public radio work.

In any event, the goal was to get the stories back into the oral tradition where they belong. Radio broadcasts are just too fleeting; you blast a five minute anecdote out into the ionosphere and hope it lands on appreciative ears. Then it's gone forever.

And a book just isn't the perfect medium for a campfire tale. The audiobook became inevitable. I would write and recite, Chris would record and add sound effects and music—but we needed a third, someone with business sense who could oversee manufacturing and bring the product to market. That role was ably filled by Fagan Hart. Things fell together and then, for a short while in 2003, it was real.

We sold about 1000 of them, and gave up. Filling orders for one, two, or three CDs at a time became just too tedious. Trying to collect money from stores who were trying to delay payment became too distasteful. And overall, we quickly recognized the labor versus profit equation was imbalanced.

Meanwhile, a lot of people who bought the CD asked, "Why don't you have this in book form?"

Well, now I do. Here are the scripts, just as I wrote and recorded them. I have added "Author's Notes" to give you extra information and a little "behind the scenes" look at each story.

And, for those equipped with the hardware and technical know-how, the CD itself is once again available for downloading. You can find it here and there on the web, but I'd encourage you to seek it out at the company who summoned it back from the dead, Crossroad Press, at www.crossroadpress.com.

Whether you choose to read it or hear it, I hope you enjoy it. And if these stories inspire a goose bump or two, that's my gift to you!

WHAT LIES BENEATH LAKE CHAMPLAIN?

Perhaps Champlain is not one of the "great lakes." It is certainly a good lake—and—at least in my estimation, one of the countries "better" lakes.

It is about 120 miles long, plunging like a dagger from Quebec and filleting Vermont from New York State. It's about 11 miles wide at its widest.

And the ever-changing surface of Lake Champlain is like a screen that conceals Vermont's oldest and most enduring mystery.

Oddly, Lake Champlain is on approximately the same latitude as the infamous "Loch Ness." That, in part, may explain why hundreds of people claim to have encountered "something mysterious" in the lake.

And that "something"—whatever it may be—is apparently alive.

In Vermont, we call it "Champ." In New York—perhaps because they are on more intimate terms with the thing—they refer to it more endearingly, as "Champy." But according to those who've come face-to-face with this aquatic giant, there really isn't anything "cute" about it.

Back in the 1960s, when I first started hearing about the Lake Champlain Monster, I didn't give it much thought. I figured it was just another supernatural story, a "dragon in the lake" sort of thing, perhaps best suited for fantasy novels and Hollywood special effects.

The picture I had in my head was of some giant supernatural creature that had been swimming around since long before the European intrusion.

Then I started studying up on it. And the whole prospect started sounding slightly more... scientific.

First of all, there have been hundreds of recorded sightings dating all the way back to when Champlain sailed down the lake in 1609.

Prior to that, the Native Americans were telling the tale. They'd sprinkle offerings—tobacco and such—in the water at Split Rock before crossing over from New York. A sort of toll, I suppose, to guarantee safe passage.

Since then there have been water sightings, land sightings... in 1973 one woman even spotted Champ from the air when she was flying over the lake in her father's plane.

Nineteenth century newspapers were full of monster stories.

For example, on August 31st, 1870 a St. Albans newspaper reported, "The What-Is-It of Lake Champlain was again interviewed near Barber's Point on Monday last. It was in full view of passengers of steamer CURLEW, and was an object projecting some distance from the water and going at railroad speed."

The newspaper was called The Temperance Advocate. And "temperance" has played a role in monster sightings for a long time.

In 1892 Captain Moses Blow, who'd worked for the Champlain Transportation Company for 42 years, was on the lake one serene summer day piloting the A. WILLIAMS.

He, his crew, and some passengers got a good look at the "serpent". It was early afternoon, some two and a half miles north of Basin Harbor. An account by Capt. Blow's daughter gives more details. She said: "They were at anchor and all of a sudden the boat started rocking, and they couldn't imagine what in the world was the matter. [They were] looking all around when all of a sudden, the head, then the neck came out of the water and it looked right straight at them, and then [Capt. Blow] said, 'Let's get out of here,' and then they headed for Burlington...."

The boat had been at anchor because, coincidentally, a group of scientists was aboard to check the depth of the lake. They'd measured to 400 feet and still hadn't reached bottom. The temperature down there was 38 degrees. The scientists told Capt. Blow that if anyone drowned there they would never come up—the pressure would hold the body in place.

A sad footnote to the story may illustrate why no monster's carcass has ever been found. Apparently Capt. Blow's brother

Charlie and nephew Harvey later drowned at that exact spot—and their bodies never surfaced.

Let's move ahead to the 20th century. On July 30, 1984, the largest mass Champ-sighting in history occurred.

It was aboard a sightseeing boat called THE SPIRIT OF ETHAN ALLEN.

On that fateful day the boat was near Appletree Point, just north of downtown Burlington. A private party was in progress, celebrating the wedding anniversary of a Massachusetts couple. It was around six o'clock in the evening. About 80 passengers were aboard.

The boat's owner, Michael Shea, is a professional airplane pilot and a keen observer—maybe that's why he was the first to spot something unusual.

He told me, "It was a perfect flat calm day on the lake. Not a ripple on the water... I saw it about 200 feet... away... [First] I thought it was a stray wake.... I stared at it awhile and noticed [whatever it was] was creating its own wake."

By the time he'd climbed to the upper deck the band had stopped playing. People were rushing to the rails to watch the humped creature swimming beside the boat. Many out-of-staters had never even heard of The Lake Champlain Monster, but they were all seeing... something.

Even the Captain saw it. And, according to Mike, "He was one of those hard people to convince of anything."

Another witness, Bette Morris of Grand Isle—daughter of the anniversary couple—anticipated the "Temperance Question" and said, "We hadn't been drinking all that much at the time, either."

The creature remained visible for about three minutes. Mike Shea said three to five humps had surfaced, each about 12 inches out of the water. He estimated the creature was about 30 feet long. It was [he said] "... green-brown [and] slimy-looking, like a frog..." It swam parallel with the boat for 1000 yards until a speedboat approached. Then the creature turned 90 degrees and submerged.

Mike recalls the image vividly. He said, "You know how when something goes underwater it turns sort of a yellowish color? Especially in this water. I could see that. It disappeared and the wake stopped."

Astonishingly, several people saw the creature reappear about 15 minutes later!

Bette Morris snapped a picture, but, like so many Champ photographs, the image proved inconclusive.

Since then Champ has been seen dozens—no doubt thousands—of times. Photos, digital images, and videotapes have been taken. Today, he's a star, having made guest appearances—in CGI form—in many television documentaries.

During his first brush with stardom, back in the early 1800s, waves of tourists flooded Lake Champlain in response to showman P.T. Barnum's offer of $50,000 for the creature—dead or alive. As far as we know the money is unclaimed.

Today, thanks to the legislatures of Vermont and New York,

Champ is a protected species, so the only things that can be shot are photographs and videos.

But I have a theory about Lake Champlain and its so-called "Monster." I believe that one protects the other. The ever-changing surface of the water is a magical veil that will never be lifted. Consequently, we will never see clearly what lies beneath.

So I also believe that one hundred years from today we'll know exactly as much about Champ as we did one hundred years ago. And every year, from Whitehall, New York to the Richelieu River, people will continue to spot that mysterious serpentine head swimming wild and unclassified, and always just slightly out of camera range.

AUTHOR'S NOTE: The "Champ Riddle" keeps people scratching their heads. Every year since this script was written more evidence has appeared, but, true to form, the animal itself remains "just slightly out of camera range".

One of the more remarkable sighting occurred in 2006 when two fishermen, Peter Bodette and Dick Affolter, managed to video something very near their boat and just under the surface. Because of the credibility of the witnesses and the quality of their video, this local story made it all the way to ABC News. I was part of a Voice of America broadcast that told the story worldwide, so I had an opportunity to meet the witnesses in person.

The short video I saw seems to show two creatures slightly below the surface of the water, and very close to a fishing boat. They look real and they are moving; one even seems to bite at the other.

Peter Bodette said the "thing" was a big around as his thigh. "I'm 100 percent sure of what we saw," he says with complete confidence, but "I'm not 100 percent sure of what it was."

Mr. Bodette's companion, Dick Affolter, an attorney, couldn't ID it either. "It just didn't fit anything—any creature I had seen."

The witnesses said that parts of it—maybe its nose or part of its head—sometimes came above the water.

The men admit that prior to their sighting they were both Champ skeptics.

Oddly, the video seems to have vanished from just about all the places it was posted on the web. Rumor has it that the complete video reveals a good deal more than the snippet that was broadcast on TV, but the witnesses won't release it without proper compensation.

Nonetheless, with much persistence and a thorough web search I discovered that it is still possible to locate the video.

More recently, in 2009, a YouTube video appeared showing a USS (Unidentified Swimming Something). The cell phone video was recorded at Oakledge Park on Sunday, May 31 at about 5:30 in the morning. It definitely shows a silhouetted something moving through the water, part in, part out. Speculation ran from a paddling dog to an adolescent moose.

The author of the video, Burlington resident, Eric Olsen, remained strangely remote, refusing to give in-depth interviews or even state what he thought he saw. "I was just filming the water," Mr. Olsen told the *Burlington Free Press,* "when, out of the corner of my eye, I saw something move, and I turned toward it and tried to zoom in on it."

See it for yourself. His video is still pretty easy to find on YouTube.

In June, 2009 I met with the source of what, for me, is the most remarkable Champ-related revelation of all time. I attended a lecture by Elizabeth von Muggenthaler, a scientist who runs Fauna Communications in Hillsborough, North Carolina.

Up until that time most, if not all, Champ encounters had been visual. But Elizabeth heard the creature. What's more, she even made an audio recording of its sound.

One chilly June morning in 2003, Liz and a team of scientists, under contract to the Discovery Channel, were visiting Lake Champlain, working on a documentary about Champ. It was eight in the morning. Everything was still. The water was mirror-smooth.

The team members, using highly sensitive underwater recording equipment, were cold, probably bored, and not too optimistic that anything remarkable would happen.

Then . . . everything changed.

Very, very faintly, an unexpected sound came over the headphones. It was not the sound of frolicking fish or outboard motors. It was something they'd never heard before in the lake. But it was definitely an animal sound.

If they'd been at sea, the series of high-pitched tickings and chirpings would have been familiar: the sounds made by dolphins or Beluga whales.

But here's the important point: only whales and dolphins are known to produce echolocation. Yet, something in Lake Champlain was unquestionably using bio-sonar. There are no known dolphins or whales in Lake Champlain. So what was making the signal?

Elizabeth believes it is the unknown creature we call Champ. She says, "This creature is unique, possibly critically endangered, and needs to be studied scientifically. Those that witness something strange on the lake, please don't be worried anymore about people thinking you are crazy."

During the week they spent on Lake Champlain they recorded the sounds in three different locations. Now new expeditions and data are on the way. So stay tuned!

By the way, Fauna Communications's website is:

www.animalvoice.com

People have asked me to tell them my favorite Champ story. I think that would have to be one that involves Burlington physician Burns Eastman, a 1911 graduate of the University of Vermont Medical College. In the early 1940s he and his wife were driving back from Canada through the Champlain Islands. It was broad daylight. The road was little-traveled in those days, so no other traffic was in sight.

The couple slowly made their way across Sand Bar Bridge, a one and a quarter mile, narrow causeway that connects South Hero with Milton. At about halfway, they had to stop. Something was in the road. A fallen log perhaps? Or maybe a gigantic piece of driftwood?

Whatever it was appeared to be from eight to ten inches thick and long enough to completely block the narrow road.

Dr. Eastman got out and approached the log. There were no guardrails on the roadside in those days, so he figured it would be fairly easy to roll it over and topple it into the lake. But he didn't have to. As Dr. Eastman and his wife stared in disbelief the "log" became animated. It slithered and flopped and finally worked its way down the side of the causeway and into the water, where it swam away.

That happened in the 1940s. No similar event is likely to happen today because the causeway is wider, more elevated, and sturdy guardrails line both sides of the road.

I like the story because it is a rare example of Champ on land. And I tend to believe it because I know the doctor's family.

Sand Bar Bridge as it appears today

DANVILLE'S DIVINE COMEDY

Sunny Italy may have produced the great poet Dante Alighieri, but it took the great state of Vermont to produce a native son like John P. Weeks.

Mr. Weeks of North Danville is a historical and literary figure who today is all but forgotten. Yet, something astoundingly strange happened to him back in July of 1838. Townspeople swore it was true. In fact, a verifying document exists, written in Mr. Weeks's own hand.

It bears the signatures of thirty-one trustworthy Vermonters, fifteen of them were eyewitnesses, including four church deacons, three ministers, and three medical doctors.

Briefly, Mr. Weeks, a 26-year-old farmer, took sick. For six days he suffered the agonies of "inflammation of the bowels"—what we now call appendicitis—and finally he died.

His relatives undressed him, beginning the process of "laying him out" in the parlor, when suddenly the dead man sat up and modestly demanded his pants.

He then jumped out of bed, walked unsteadily to the door and stood there transfixed, waving.

And there our story might have ended. But it seems there was a lot more yet to unfold.

After his health had fully returned, Mr. Weeks wrote a narrative explaining everything that had happened between the time the doctor pronounced him dead and the moment he sat up looking for his trousers.

Apparently he had taken a trip through Heaven and Hell in the company of an angel.

His description is perhaps less complete than Dante's, but John P. Weeks saw Heaven as only a Vermont farmer might. He wrote: "The land of Paradise is perfectly level, grass perhaps half an inch high, no trees nor stumps nor stones."

He also said the "climate was delightful" and the air, he said, was "always agreeable."

The layout of Heaven seemed to resemble that of a typical

Vermont town. In the same way there's a Danville, a North Danville, West Danville, and South Danville, Mr. Weeks's Heaven is similarly subdivided.

East Heaven, he said, is full of singing angels and a "Third Heaven"—perhaps "North Heaven"—was where God kept his golden throne.

Mr. Weeks also got a good look at "that other place" where, he wrote, "I saw a multitude that no man could number, in a dark, lost condition. They were weeping and wailing and trying to climb out... only to fall back again."

The angel told John to be sure to warn all sinners not to come to that place of torment.

John readily agreed, so they headed directly back to North Danville where John P. Weeks was restored to life. After that, he spent his 44 remaining years telling people about his tour of Heaven and Hell and warning sinners to avoid that hot and hopeless place he had seen on his way to and from Paradise.

AUTHOR'S NOTE: The strange tale of John P. Weeks is one of those little-known Vermont classics. It might have been forgotten entirely if Mr. Weeks had not written his lengthy account of the affair. Last I knew, the original is filed away in the Vermont Historical Society.

Although John died for the second and final time in 1882, he had fathered fifteen children, some of whom lived to keep the tale alive.

In 1890 it was published in a 41 page booklet titled *The Narrative of Bro. John P. Weeks.* It's hard to find today because only 150 copies were printed for Peter Connal, ESQ by S.C. O'Connor of Newport.

Although the "Weeks Miracle" occurred a good ten years before the advent of Modern American Spiritualism, the Spirtualists embraced the story as evidence of their beliefs. Mr. Weeks's account of his near-death experiences and chats with the dead were published in a number of Spirtualist publications, including *The World's Paper,* circa 1887.

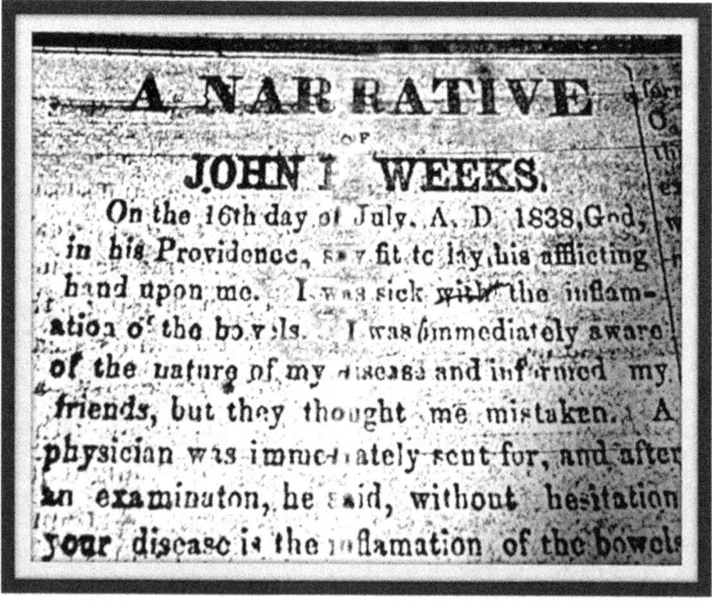

A NARRATIVE
OF
JOHN I WEEKS.

On the 16th day of July, A. D. 1838, God, in his Providence, saw fit to lay his afflicting hand upon me. I was sick with the inflam-ation of the bowels. I was immediately aware of the nature of my disease and informed my friends, but they thought me mistaken. A physician was immediately sent for, and after an examinaton, he said, without hesitation your disease is the inflamation of the bowels

In 1966 Tennie Gaskill Toussaint, who lived in that neck of the woods, wrote an account for the short-lived *Vermonter* magazine. In it she was able to record some recollections from the locals. She wrote, "Elderly people of North Danville still tell about how their great-grandfather or grandmother was living at the time John P. Weeks was sick and died—went to Heaven—caught a horrible glimpse of Hell—and came back to earth and to life again, to live many more years."

"O yes it was true," neighbors said. "A lot of [people] were in the sick room and saw him die, and knew when he came back to life again. Doctors and ministers from all around testified to the fact."

I first learned of the story around 1993 when I was researching my book *Green Mountain Ghosts, Ghouls & Unsolved Mysteries.* As I recall I was sitting on the floor of the Fletcher Free Library in Burlington thumbing through vintage 1950s editions of the publications of the Vermont Folklore Society.

I immediately loved the tale, told it on public radio, and included it in my book.

For those who like clear-cut endings to tales such as this one, Mr. Weeks and most of his family are buried in the Ward cemetery in North Danville.

J. P. WEEKS
BORN
DEC. 26, 1812
DIED
JUNE 21, 1882

COW KILL - A SHOCKING TALE

These grisly events occurred at a deceptively tranquil Vermont farm, a place scenic enough to grace any postcard or promotional calendar.

It was winter again. The wet, foggy night of February 14, 1984—the early hours of Valentine's Day.

The scene of the crime—an innocent-looking barn—was part of Honeymoon Valley Farm, a successful dairy operation beautifully situated in Dummerston, Vermont, between Route 5 and the Connecticut River. Owned by Robert Ranney and his wife Judy, the farm was hardly the sort of place to be visited by anything... unnatural.

Yet Mr. Ranney discovered a terrifying tragedy unlike anything he'd ever seen before. At about three o'clock in the morning, as always, he headed out after the milking cows. As he walked past the barn where the heifers were kept, something caught his eye.

He said, "I saw one heifer that looked like she might need help . . . And I looked in the barn...."

What he saw was a nightmarish tableau, a gruesome sight the memory of which would be with him the rest of his life.

Twenty-three of his 29 heifers were dead. No blood. No wounds. No sign of a struggle. Just dead.

How could it be? Only a few hours earlier all the little animals had been perfectly all right.

And now, according to one account, they were lying in a perfect circle with feed still in their mouths.

When he'd recovered from the shock, the first thing Mr. Ranney did was call his veterinarian. After examining the corpses, the vet couldn't escape an odd conclusion: the animals had been electrocuted. But try as he might, he couldn't figure out how it had happened.

They had died instantly, he assured Mr. Ranney; none of them had suffered. He could determine this because there were no signs of a struggle nor evidence the cows had tried to escape. Whatever happened must have happened very fast—instantly—making the deaths even more of a puzzle.

Because of the value of the livestock—worth over a thousand dollars a head—an insurance investigator came to inspect the scene. He agreed that all 23 cows had died instantly, probably by electrocution. He added that the killings could not have been achieved intentionally, nor with such precision. Thus, he had ruled out foul play... but it didn't look like an accident either.

So suddenly the events took on an added layer of mystery.

Then more investigators checked the scene, including electricians, but no one could discover a reason for the eerie electrical deaths.

Mr. Ranney voiced a theory of his own, saying, "What it looked like was lightning... I've seen plenty of cows hit by lightning out in the field, and that's what these cows looked like."

But there were absolutely no signs of a strike: the barn door remained closed, there were no scorch marks on the roof, beams, or floor, and none of the hay had ignited. More telling, perhaps, is that none of the dead cows had split hoofs. Lightning will generally leave that mark if no other.

So what happened?

The most bizarre theory was put forth several days later by another examiner, an ex-policeman from Rutland, named William Chapleau. Mr. Chapleau inspected the scene on behalf of a private investigative organization called MUFON, an acronym for Mutual UFO Network.

While scanning the area with a Geiger counter, he found high radiation at the center of the barn and in the cornfield where the cows had been buried.

Noting the proximity of the farm to the Vermont Yankee Nuclear Power Plant in Vernon, Mr. Chapleau's first guess was that the animals had been killed by some kind of freak radioactive discharge. He soon learned, however, that Yankee had been shut down at the time.

Then—having eliminated all other possibilities to his own satisfaction—Mr. Chapleau ventured that the animals may have been killed... by a UFO.

On the night the cows died, four people had contacted him about a "torpedo-shaped" UFO over the Vernon Nuclear Plant. Also, a mysterious ball of light had been seen that same night in nearby Hinsdale, N.H.

According to Mr. Chapleau, no other explanation for the strange deaths has ever emerged.

Nearly thirty years have passed and still there is no solution to this odd barnyard mystery. But there is a chilling footnote to the tale.

The burial of the 23 cows had been unceremonious. They simply bulldozed a big hole in the field, pushed the bodies into it, and covered them with dirt.

Then they planted corn over everything.

But, as weird as it sounds, not corn, not grass, not anything at all, has ever grown on the circle that defines the dead cows' grave.

AUTHOR'S NOTE: Every now and then, just when I think I've put one of these Vermont mysteries to rest, some new bit of information comes along, often adding a little chill to already baffling circumstances.

And sometimes that chill comes from an unexpected place in an unexpected manner.

The "Cow Kill" events took place in 1984.

Almost 10 years later, when I researched the incident, I used three difference sources for the story: *The Brattleboro Reformer*, *The Rutland Herald*, and Robert Ellis Cahill's book *New England's*

Visitors From Outer Space. Of course I wanted to interview the family but learned they had left the Dummerston area and I was unable to find their new address.

On October 21, 1994, while I was appearing on Tim Philbin's radio show in Middlebury, we were discussing this incident. After the show, as I was leaving the studio, the receptionist said, "There's a lady waiting to see you in the other room."

That's weird, I thought.

I walked into the waiting area where I was met by a woman who introduced herself as "The Cow Lady". It was Mrs. Ranney, wife of the farmer who owned the electrocuted cows.

Understandably taken aback, I greeted her warmly and told her how I'd wanted to meet her but hadn't been able to locate the family.

She explained that they had left Dummerston and relocated to a small farming community near Middlebury. Coincidently, she had been driving by and had heard me on the radio telling her story. An odd bit of synchronicity! Why not stop in, she thought.

I must admit I was a little worried about some kind of confrontation. To head it off I quickly asked her if I had reported the details accurately. Yes, in general I had, she told me. However, I got the dates wrong. I had said the tragedy happened on February 16, 1984. In reality, it was February 14th—St. Valentine's Day.

I'm thinking, Ahh, a great addition to the story.

Fearing my sources had messed up or exaggerated other details, I asked her if, by now, the mysterious deaths had been scientifically and satisfactorily explained.

No, she said, it is as much a mystery today as it was the night it happened. In ten years no realistic theory—including stray voltage—has ever been offered.

Then she told me one chilling additional detail. Something non-supernatural, but altogether human. She told me how much the family had been upset by the animal deaths. The Ranney children especially had loved the little cows and viewed them almost like pets. They even had names for them. They were devastated by the tragedy.

This is the sort of detail I often overlook. I can get completely wrapped us in the bizarre and mysterious aspects of a situation and I ignore, or I'm insensitive to, the more important, all-too-human side.

I must never lose sight of the fact that, above all, these are stories about people.

UVM'S TENURED TERRORS

At Burlington's University of Vermont, the idea of "School Spirit" takes on an all new meaning. At least 18 buildings on campus—and not just residence halls—seem to have ghosts living in them.

You might say that UVM is something of a Ghostly Ghetto... and I'm the census-taker.

There's a haunted fraternity, a haunted sorority, several haunted dormitories, including Redstone, Coolidge, Millis, and the most infamous of the lot, Converse Hall.

That's where UVM's best known spirit—the venerable "Henry"—seems to eternally reside.

To me Converse looks very much like Castle Frankenstein. It's a massive, brooding, ivy-cloaked structure, built as a men's dormitory in 1895.

Henry showed up in the 1920s. Said to be a reclusive, overburdened and highly stressed medical student, poor Henry was failing academically and socially. Profoundly melancholic, he hanged himself in the attic.

Today he's dead but not gone. Since Henry's demise, strange things have happened in the ancient rooms and corridors of Converse. Doors mysteriously open and shut. Possessions vanish. Bewildered students discover their locked rooms have been rearranged.

And a certain rocking chair is seen to rock... all by itself.

A young woman told me about the time she went alone to a study room, turned on the lights, and began working at one of the carrels.

Suddenly she heard the tattoo of typing several desks over.

The room had been dark when she entered; she'd seen no one come in, yet the typing continued. Puzzled, she got up and followed the sound to the desk where the noise seemed to originate. No one was there.

Henry, preparing for some "final exam," perhaps?

One night another Converse resident was disturbed by the sensation of someone stroking her face. Frightened, she woke her husband who groggily insisted it was just a dream.

When they were almost asleep again, a crash jolted them fully awake. The wall mirror lay shattered on the floor. The frightened couple couldn't understand how the heavy mirror had fallen; it had been bolted to the wall. The mystery deepened when they saw its four bolts were still securely in place.

An oddly poignant story involves a female student whose mother passed away.

Following the funeral the young woman returned to Converse. Upon entering her locked room she found everything soaking wet: furniture, clothing, even the walls themselves. There was simply no explanation.

Someone said it was as if the walls themselves had been weeping for the girl's loss.

More likely it was Henry.

In general, he seems to plague women more than men, but perhaps that's predictable behavior from an eternally adolescent male.

Though most people consider Henry a ghost, for him it must be some kind of hell. Imagine being condemned to spend all eternity in school.

Then there's Grasse Mount, the elegant, two story federal mansion at 411 Main Street. Built in 1804 by Thaddeus Tuttle, this Burlington landmark was a private home, changing hands several times before UVM bought it in 1895.

Many people agree that someone, or something, benign but excitable, lurks within its walls.

When Continuing Education was there during the 1980s, most of the ghostly goings on occurred upstairs.

Susan, the financial manager, was working alone one evening in 1984. Doors were locked, windows closed and secured for the night.

She was the only living soul in the building—or so she thought.

Between 8:00 and 9:00 o'clock something happened. Susan said, "The windows in the window jams just started to go back and forth—a huge rattling. I could see the motion, but there was nothing there."

"Wind" might be the immediate explanation, but Susan says no. "It was still light outside," she told me. "I could see there was no wind. I'm a windsurfer, so I'm always looking for that."

Over the next couple of hours the commotion escalated. The heating system began clanking and banging—the familiar cacophony of ancient plumbing. Trouble is, it was summer and the heat was turned off.

"I stayed there an hour and a half, maybe two," Susan told me. "I walked out of the room when the windows were beating themselves back and forth. I said, Okay, you can have the building. I can't concentrate any longer."

Lynne Ballard, former interim director of Continuing Education, recalls a similar evening. Around midnight the silence was broken by loud noises upstairs: doors slamming, drawers banging, footsteps pounding. Fearing vandals—but secretly suspecting the ghost—she phoned her husband Bill, a senior campus administrator. Though skeptical about ghostly noisemakers, Bill arrived to find the commotion so active, loud, and unsettling that he summoned Security.

The officers arrived, searched, and left, finding nothing.

Though embarrassed, Bill was far less skeptical about the invisible realm.

The most dramatic of UVM spirits have not only been sensed, and heard... but seen.

UVM's spectral superstar resides at 146 South Williams Street. It's an old brick mansion that for years was a private residence, until it was acquired by the school.

Many people tell of mysterious after-hours experiences. In the mid-70s a secretary was working alone on Saturday afternoon.

Around four she heard the front door open and close. Footsteps climbed the stairs.

She called, "Hello," but no one responded.

Later, she asked a visiting student to go upstairs and see who'd come in. He checked thoroughly... but found no one.

A janitor mopping floors one dark morning was startled when something unseen knocked his bucket over, sloshing dirty water everywhere. As he tried to determine what had happened, overhead lights began flashing. He actually saw the light switch flipping up and down. Immediately he put in for a transfer.

Richard Does, former director of Counseling and Testing, had the most unsettling encounter.

One evening while alone in his office, he saw "a spectral image gliding down the stairway."

He observed it clearly and described it this way: it was "... an elderly man with distinct facial features and a bulbous nose." A receding hairline and thick sideburns framed the apparition's angry expression. No hands or feet were visible at the ends of his old-fashioned jacket and trousers.

Dr. Does said the entire figure was "...kind of translucent and shimmering like a jellyfish."

Before drifting away, the specter glowered directly at Dr. Does as if to ask, Just what are you doing here, mister?

Dr. Does asked himself the same question... and left.

Many people working alone in the building have heard the conventional sounds of a ghost: footsteps, doors, and the like. But this building offers something unique: sneezes and coughs, suggesting we'll all have ghostly germs and viruses waiting for us when we reach the spirit world.

So who is haunting 146 South Williams Street? Perhaps it's the spirit of Capt. John Nabb, a colorful seafarer who lived there in the 19th century.

Or maybe it's Prof. Eldridge Jacobs, a UVM geologist who died in 1957.

For some reason folks have taken to calling the ghost "Captain Jacobs," adding more confusion to this already perplexing subject.

AUTHOR'S NOTE: Just as the number of UVM's student body increases year after year, so does their ghost population. Since 1994, when I first wrote about UVM's ghosts, I keep hearing about more haunted buildings.

In fact, some years ago the alumni magazine contracted with me to do a census of UVM ghosts. At that time I identified seventeen structures with ghost stories attached; now there are more. Because UVM tends to play musical buildings, a place's purpose may have been reassigned by the time you read this, but the building itself will still be the same and presumably its ghost will still be in residence:

1. Clement House, 194 South Prospect Street (part of "Admissions")
2. Booth House, 86 South Williams Street
3. Bittersweet House, 151 Prospect Street
4. Continuing Education, 322 South Prospect Street
5. Converse Hall, 75 Colchester Ave.
6. Coolidge Hall, 402 South Prospect Street (on Redstone Campus)
7. Grasse Mount, 411 Main Street
8. Jacobs House, 146 South Williams Street
9. Lamba Iota fraternity, 440 Pearl Street
10. Millis Hall, 67 Spear Street
11. Old Mill, on the Green
12. Pi Beta Phi sorority, 369 South Prospect
13. Redstone Hall, on the Redstone Campus
14. Simpson Hall, on Redstone Campus
15. University's Farm House (Spear Street used for agricultural studies)
16. Wheeler House, 133 South Prospect Street
17. 481 Main Street (site of an exorcism)
18. Mabel Louise Southwick Memorial, 392 South Prospect Street

Newer research will probably reveal additional haunts because "The Ghost Machine" continues to produce. Years pass, people die, new students arrive, more stories get told.

THE BENNINGTON TRIANGLE

In this story we move from haunted houses, to haunted heights—the untamed wilderness of Glastonbury Mountain.

Located in the Green Mountains near Bennington, the area has always had a "reputation." It's inaccessible, remote, full of dark places, jutting outcroppings, vast marshlands and quiet pools.

Since pre-colonial times there have been strange tales of mysterious lights, untraceable sounds, and unidentifiable odors. Supposedly specters skulked among the trees. And unknown creatures—glimpsed fleetingly within the silent swampland—burned themselves forever into memory.

Native Americans shunned the place, believing the land was cursed.

The few colonial families who settled there were plagued by misfortune: recurring bouts of inexplicable illness; too many deaths in childbirth; and madness claimed more than its share of victims.

It was on those sinister slopes that, in the early 19th century, a coach full of travelers was attacked by the baffling "Bennington Monster." And there, in 1892, Henry MacDowell went haywire and murdered Jim Crowley. Sentenced to life in the Waterbury Asylum, he escaped and vanished. Some say he returned to the Glastenbury wilds, where he remains to this day.

But all this happened a long time ago.

Today the mountains are no less mysterious, and dark tales are still told.

However, there's one thing we know for sure: Glastenbury Mountain is the site of a terrifying mystery. And it happened not too long ago.

I refer to the events as "The Bennington Triangle" because they involve a series of unexplained disappearances—perhaps ten in all. Beginning late in 1945 a number of people simply stepped off the face of the earth.

The strangeness started with a man named Middie Rivers, a 75 year old hunting and fishing guide.

Native to the region, Mr. Rivers led four hunters up the mountain on November 12, 1945.

Returning to camp, he got a bit ahead of the others. They never caught up. Somehow, the guide had vanished completely.

Volunteers and police combed the area for a month. They never lost hope because Mr. Rivers was an experienced woodsman; he'd know how to survive in the wild.

But no trace—nothing—was ever found.

A young woman named Paula Welden was the second to go.

On Sunday, December 6, 1946, this 18 year old Bennington College sophomore set out for a short hike on the Long Trail.

When Monday afternoon came, Paula hadn't returned. The 5'5" blonde should have been easy to spot in her bright red parka when the Sheriff's Department was joined by 400 students, faculty, and townspeople.

The Governor called in the FBI. New York and Connecticut State Police joined the hunt. Search parties combed the area for weeks. In spite of their efforts, a $5,000 reward, and the aid of a famous clairvoyant, not a single clue turned up.

REWARD, $5,000.00 IF FOUND ALIVE

MISSING PERSON

REWARD, $2,000.00 IF FOUND DEAD

Specimen of Handwriting and Printing

P. Welden
Bennington College
Bennington
Vt.

Paula Jean Welden, 18 yrs. 5'5", 122 lbs., blond hair, long bob, blue eyes, fair complexion with much color, features regular, nose slightly "turned up", cleft in chin. Grayish scar on left knee, vaccination mark right thigh, small scar above left eye under eyebrow. Walks with a long springy step, has erect carriage. Athletic type.

DENTAL CHART ON BACK OF CIRCULAR

PAULA JEAN WELDEN

Paula Jean Welden, Brookdale Road, Stamford, Conn. a student at Bennington College, Bennington, Vermont, disappeared from college on the afternoon of December 1, 1946. When last seen she was wearing a red parka jacket with fur trimmed hood, blue jeans, white sneakers with heavy soles named Top-Sider, size 6½ or 7, and a small gold Elgin ladies' wrist watch with narrow black band. This watch has repairer's marking, 13050 HD, scratched on the inside of back case. This girl likes skating, bicycling, hiking, camping, swimming, square dancing and playing the guitar. She is an art student interested in water colors, oils, pencil and charcoal sketching, and has assisted a mural painter and done illustrations (black and white). She has also done waitress work.

REWARD, LIVING OR DEAD, $5,000.000 IF FOUND ALIVE, $2,000.00 IF FOUND DEAD. $5,000.00 reward for information leading to the whereabouts of Paula Jean Welden and resulting in her being found alive. $2,000.00 reward for information leading to the whereabouts of Paula Jean Welden and resulting in the identification of her body. Reward expires July 1, 1947.

Please forward any information to girl's father, Mr. W. Archibald Welden Brookdale Road, Stamford, Connecticut.

The official search—involving bloodhounds, airplanes, helicopters, and well over 1000 people—ended on December 22 with no results. No sign of a body. No clothing. No evidence at all. The only thing certain is that a young woman took a walk in the Vermont hills and never came back.

Oddly, the third person vanished on the third anniversary of Paula Welden's disappearance—three years to the day.

Elderly James E. Tedford left his relatives in St. Albans. His family put him on a bus for the Bennington Soldiers Home, where he lived.

He never arrived. The exact location of his disappearance is uncertain. Witnesses saw him get on the bus. He was aboard at the stop before Bennington. But, impossible as it sounds, he apparently never got off!

Again, no clues. No one saw anything. Even the bus driver was baffled.

Soldier's Home

On Columbus Day of 1950 it was eight-year-old Paul Jepson's turn.

His mother and father were farmers and caretakers of the town dump. That's where the tragedy occurred.

Paul waited in the pickup while his mother relocated some pigs. She only left him for a moment. But when she looked up, Paul was gone.

Well-practiced volunteers commenced another search. Hundreds of civilians joined officials to comb the dump, the road, and the mountains.

This time they instituted a "double check" system: as soon as one group finished searching an area, a second group inspected the same area.

Coast Guard planes and local psychics proved useless.

Fact or legend, I can't say, but I remember reading that the blood-hounds lost Paul's scent at the junction of East and Chapel Roads—the exact spot where Paula Welden was last seen.

VERMONT POLICE CONTINUE SEARCH FOR MISSING BOY

Two weeks later Freida Langer was hiking with her cousin near their camp on the Glastonbury slopes. Freida was an experienced gun-handler and woodsperson. She was thoroughly familiar with the area.

At about 3:45 p.m., only about half a mile from camp, she

slipped and fell into a stream. Her cousin waited while Freida ran the short distance back to change clothes.

But she never returned. And she never reached camp. And no one saw her come out of the woods.

Again, another month-long search involving helicopters, amphibious planes, and hordes of people on foot.

Again nothing.

The Bennington Banner wrote, "One of the things hard to explain is how Mrs. Langer could have become so completely lost in an hour's time before dark in an area with which she was so thoroughly familiar."

On December 3, 1950, only a few days after the search for Freida Langer ended, Frances Christman left her home to visit a friend just one-half mile away.

Somewhere on that brief hike she vanished without a trace.

Think about it. Six people disappeared between 1945 and 1950. Simply blinked out of existence. Where did they go? How can we possibly explain it?

And . . . was it only six?

In a *Burlington Free Press* article dated 10-25-81, reporter Sally Jacobs says that two years after the Paula Welden disappearance, "a trio of hunters from Massachusetts vanished near [the ghost town of] Glastenbury. Their disappearance, like those that preceded them, remains a mystery."

And one of *The Bennington Banner* articles I reviewed made reference to a thirteen-year-old Bennington boy, Melvin Hills, who was lost in the same area around October 11, 1942.

If these are true, then the number of disappearances goes from six to ten.

Where did they go? How can we possibly explain such a thing?

Did the so-called "Bennington Monster" carry them off into the caves and swamps of Glastonbury Mountain?

Could they have tumbled through some interdimensional

trapdoor, some northern equivalent of the Bermuda Triangle?

Did tiny, melon-headed aliens whisk them off to some faraway planet?

Or maybe they encountered a certain enchanted stone, known to the Indians for yawning and swallowing anyone who steps on it?

A *Bennington Banner* reporter even speculated that there exists something of a Yankee Shangri-La upon Glastenbury Mountain, a lost horizon into which people inadvertently step, never to be seen again.

To some that may seem the best explanation, because it discounts less happy endings.

For example, there is a far more prosaic possibility: something not precisely defined in the annals of American crime circa 1945—the serial killer.

The Bennington events took place over a limited amount of time: five years. And in roughly the same area. The victims' ages spanned from eight to seventy-five. They were about equally divided between men and women. All occurred during the last three months of the calendar year, then stopped.

Serial killers operate that way; they do their dirty work, then drift from place to place. Maybe the perpetrator was someone who visited Vermont in October, November, and December. Maybe for hunting season, or for the holidays.

But the truth is, no murder was ever proven.

There is, however, one especially disturbing addendum to the events: On May 12, 1951 the body of Freida Langer did appear, seven months after she'd vanished!

Impossibly, the corpse was discovered among tall grasses near Somerset Reservoir. Right out in an open, perfectly visible in an area where searchers simply could not have missed it. Remember, teams had repeatedly combed the area for weeks. The search for Freida Langer was, arguably, the most thorough of all.

Unfortunately, Ms. Langer's fate couldn't be determined by examining her remains; as the *Bennington Banner* reported, they were in "gruesome condition."

And what of the others? No human remains were ever found. No thread of clothing. No blood. No hair. No clue at all.

And no reasonable explanation has even been articulated.

AUTHOR'S NOTE: In 1992, during a commentary on public radio, I coined the term "Bennington Triangle". Admittedly it was a rip-off term, derived from "Burmuda Triangle," but I wanted to convey, in modern parlance, just how weird that area around Glastenbury Mountain is reputed to be. I followed the commentary with a few book chapters and magazine articles, and, little by little, Vermonters became aware that we have a historic Neverland in our midst.

Thanks to the internet, the term and the story, quickly went

viral. As I write this I checked with Google and it returned about 803,000 results for "Bennington Triangle". On a monthly basis I get at least one and maybe more calls from TV or radio shows who want to do a story on the Triangle.

I've stopped doing them. There is too much sensationalizing and not enough investigation. Reputable print journalism is where the answers will eventually come out. So far, I have just highlighted the questions.

I sometimes get letters and email from people who have theories about what happened to the vanished hikers. UFO abductions. Satanist cults. Human sacrifice. And after that the suggestions start getting preposterous.

The Paula Weldon case seems to hold a special fascination for people. Occasionally I'm approached with secret and privileged inside information. Last time, I think, Paula's remains were in the trunk of some car, rusted and long-abandoned by the side of the Long Trail. I also heard she was buried beneath the floor of a cabin. This one was supposedly a death-bed confession and therefore true. Alas, in each case there are more reasons not to believe than to believe.

Over the years I have also been contacted by three different cold case investigators. Each was an earnest military retiree who had no personal connection to the case. One later committed suicide (I suspect no causal relationship). One vanished (meaning I think he lost interest and went on to investigate something else). And the third says he has solved the Paula Weldon case. Now we are all waiting for the big revelation.

The disappearances in and of themselves are fascinating and could solidify into a myth all their own. But when you throw in various other ingredients, fantasy elements such as Indian curses, giant unknown animals, UFOs, and even ghosts, you have a grand tale of high adventure and mystery that is just a little closer to reality than a piece of literary fiction or a TV show. After all, you can actually go there, tromp around, talk to people who know the stories. In effect, you can live the adventure.

Lately the legend of "The Bennington Triangle" has been

kept alive by a series of made-to-video films, most in the "Blair Witch" style. Many of them can be viewed on YouTube.

In the last decade or so, the reality of the situation has been punched-up by what seem to be a series of Bigfoot encounters. I talk about them at some length in my book *Vermont's Haunts,* but briefly:

In September, 2003 Ray Dufresne was headed north on Route 7 between Bennington and Manchester when he noticed something moving in a narrow, deserted field on his right. In a recent interview he told me, "It was a big black hairy thing, walking strangely. Long hairy arms; the body was huge. It was a lot bigger than me. I'm 220, so this must have been over 270. A lot over. Over 6 feet. Wider. Beefier. I just couldn't believe it."

Ray lost sight of it as it moved east into the woods of Glastenbury Mountain, considered by many to be the epicenter of the Bennington Triangle.

Mr. Dufresne's tale was buttressed when other people reported similar sightings in the same area. A week earlier, as he was driving toward Bennington College, writer Doug Dorst spotted a similar creature. And two women—Sadelle Wiltshire and Ann Mrowicki—said they had also seen the "beast" the same night as Mr. Dufresne.

Though these are just threads in the whole Bennington Triangle Tapestry, they help to complete the mysterious picture and go a long way in keeping the entire legend alive.

Such tales, hovering between history, hype, and hyperbole may be—at least to some—of questionable value. For example, Bennington history buff Tyler Resch dismisses the whole Bennington Triangle saga. He was quoted in The Bennington Banner as saying, "Almost all of this is undocumented nonsense and serves to enhance the royalties of writers (like Citro)."

He's wrong, of course. It's all documented. And I don't know that collecting a state's folklore is nonsense. If we can spark curiosity in minds, young or old, that a good thing. Better yet, if such tales motivate people to explore the history, filet the fact from the fiction, and maybe even solve the mysteries, how can that be malevolent?

Without such tales and the interest and curiosity they inspire, people like Middie Rivers (whose family thanked me for including him in my books), Jim Crowley, Freida Langer, Paula Weldon, and all the others might slip forever from memory.

To me that would be the worst thing of all.

EMILY'S BRIDGE

To the eye, the Gold Brook Bridge in Stowe is not unlike any of the scenic covered bridges that span Vermont waterways.

Some sources say this one-lane, fifty-foot structure is the oldest covered bridge in the country. Its builder, John N. Smith of Moscow, Vermont designed it with many unique features and bragged that it would last forever. Maybe he was right; today, as a historic structure, it's guaranteed perpetual care.

What better place for an eternal spirit to take up residence?

Though its formal name is "The Gold Brook Bridge," some call it "The Stowe Hollow Bridge." But to most locals, it will always be "Emily's Bridge," because Emily is the ghost who haunts it.

Scores of people have had run-ins with Emily. Some are willing to talk about it. Some won't. Perhaps it depends on the nature of the encounter—they range from benign to terrifying.

At the least menacing end of the scare spectrum we find tourists with cameras. Often photographs taken on the bridge don't come out when there's no good reason for it. Or the photographer might discover that an otherwise perfect print includes a puzzling, blurry blemish that wasn't there when the photo was snapped.

In a recent case, I received a photo from a newly-married couple who had honeymooned in Vermont. Their photo showed the bridge with a young girl standing in front of it.

"She looks perfectly human to me," I told the photographer.

"But she wasn't there when I took the picture," he said. "I was shooting the bridge. Because it was pretty. If she'd been in the way, I wouldn't have snapped the picture."

Other witnesses actually see things on the bridge, things they can't explain, like flashing white lights with no visible source.

Sometimes the point of contact is not the eye but the ear.

Certain visitors swear they can hear an eerie voice from nowhere uttering words that can't quite be understood. When the voice is understood, it sounds like a woman... crying for help.

These two varieties of encounter combined in the early seventies. Lifelong Stowe resident Ed Rhodes told me about the time he and a friend were chasing thunderstorms. Resting in the shelter of Emily's Bridge, they waited for the storm to pass. There in the semi-darkness, Ed's friend became unaccountably frightened. "Let's get out of here," he said. "I heard somebody hollering for help."

The friend started to drive away but Ed stopped him. "Wait a minute," he said. "Maybe somebody really needs help."

When they turned around, Ed saw what he described as "little tiny specks of light, like strobe lights. But," he said, "the funny thing was, the lights did not illuminate the interior of the bridge."

Sometimes the spectral contacts are a little more physical.

Hats can be whisked away when the air is absolutely still. People might experience warm spots in the dead of winter, or inexplicable chills in the blistering summer heat. One man even saw hand prints materialize on the foggy windshield of his car. A neat little trick considering there were no hands visible while the prints appeared.

Judging by these reports, you might think Emily is simply trying to get people's attention. But there are more menacing encounters, terrifying dramas played out in the dark interior of the bridge. Perhaps these actions reveal Emily's true nature.

For years—until it was stolen—a quaint "Speed Limit" sign on the bridge read, "Horses at a walk. Motor vehicles, 10 miles per hr." At such conservative velocity horses and automobiles were easy prey for Emily's assaults. Sometimes animals crossing the bridge at night were slashed by sharp invisible claws that left long bloody gashes.

When cars replaced horses, Emily continued her attacks. Her phantom claws ruined more than one perfect paint job.

So who is this strange lingering soul who hasn't quite made it across the bridge and into the afterlife?

Sadly, we don't know much about her. While many accounts say that Emily died by her own hand, most agree her tragedy occurred on that bridge around 1849.

Judging from her postmortem activities, Emily's spirit seems angry, maybe even insane.

But why?

The best known history of the haunted bridge holds that Emily was a young Stowe woman who fell in love with a man, who—for whatever reason—failed to pass muster with her family. Forbidden to marry, the love-struck youngsters decided to elope. They planned to meet on the bridge at midnight.

The appointed hour came and went, but the young man never showed. Shattered, Emily didn't know what to do. She couldn't run away alone. Nor could she return home to her "I-told-you-so" parents.

Perhaps overreacting a bit, the distraught young woman hanged herself from a rafter. And her desperate, angry ghost has haunted the bridge ever since. No doubt she's waiting for her lover to return.

There are variations of the story, of course, though all involve Emily's violent death at the Stowe Hollow Bridge. But in reality no one—psychic, scientist, nor historian—has been able to prove that Emily actually lived. Or died. We must remember, however, that in the old days families routinely buried their dead at home. Records—even death records—were not always filed. Sometimes families might choose not to talk about a death—especially a suicide.

Wherever truth lies, one thing is certain: Emily's bridge (and the area around it) generates more reports of seemingly paranormal phenomena than any other place in Vermont. Is the spirit of sad, lost Emily eternally waiting there for her lover to return? Or are the mysterious events at Stowe Hollow attributable to something else? Something stranger?

Who can say?

Looking for answers, I have visited Emily's Bridge many times over the years. Unfortunately, I've never seen anything peculiar nor have I felt as if I were in the presence of something supernatural.

I must admit I am disappointed. I guess I am not the young man Emily is waiting for.

AUTHOR'S NOTE: "Emily's Bridge" is probably the most popular and prolific paranormal attraction in Vermont. More than any other Vermont haunt, it has been featured in magazine articles, webpages, books of ghost stories, and TV spots.

Even Middle Schoolers love the story, as I have discovered repeatedly in my classroom visits. I suspect it is not the ghost, but the story, that makes Emily memorable. It's a love story that goes wrong; everyone can identify and empathize.

It is a little more difficult to explain why Emily's Bridge continues to provoke more odd incidents than any other spot in Vermont, but it is a fact.

Perhaps because the story is so well known, and because the bridge is so easily accessible that it simply has more visitors than any other haunted spot. It is even featured on Stowe's town tourist map. More visitors equals more opportunities for an experience... not to mention more exposure to suggestible individuals.

I have seen some of the evidence of these "supernatural confrontations": hard-to-explain photos and videos, recordings of anomalous sounds, unmanageable amounts of witness testimony, and countless secondhand tales.

I almost had a personal encounter with Emily, which I describe in *Vermont's Haunts*.

Overall, though, my theory is that Emily is a fiction.

No one has ever been able to prove that "Emily" ever existed. Therefore I must conclude that the ghost story is a contrivance, developed bit by bit over the years and retrofit to explain all the mysterious happenings that actually have occurred in the area around (and on) Stowe Hollow Bridge.

So, it is my belief that Emily's is not a haunted bridge. Rather, I suggest the bridge in within a haunted area—one of those inexplicable "window areas", like the Bennington Triangle, where strange things happen, and have happened, over the years.

See also *Vermont's Haunts* by Joseph A. Citro. Crossroad Press, 2012.

WINDSOR'S WATER SPRITE

This next story is a little hard to categorize.

All I can tell you for sure is that something extraordinarily weird got into a Windsor, Vermont home back in 1955.

I suppose it could have been a ghost of some little-know variety. Maybe it was a so-called poltergeist—or maybe even some kind of mischievous demon.

But to this day its identity—indeed everything about it—remains among Vermont's greatest unsolved mysteries.

Whenever I'm invited to speak about my explorations into the odder side of Vermont life, someone invariably asks me to identify the strangest thing I've come across.

People like to think in superlatives, I guess. So I try to respond that way.

Trouble is, with this story, I'm never sure which superlative to use. It isn't "horrifying" or even "scary" in any conventional sense. But when I discovered it a few years ago, I was convinced then, as I am now, that it is one of the oddest, most offbeat, and puzzling things I've ever run across.

And I assure you this is no legend or myth. I've spoken to witnesses. I've interviewed one of the family members. I'm completely satisfied that it is absolutely true.

Now most anomalies fall readily into classifiable types: ghosts, monsters, UFOs, haunted houses, psychic experiences and so on. Occasionally, however, something so monumentally strange comes along that it's completely unclassifiable. The Windsor mystery is such an event.

A physician, his wife and their two daughters had lived for

nine years in their comfortable two-story home on Cherry Street. There was nothing odd about the house itself. In fact, it could not have been more normal with its brown shingled exterior, white trim, and attached garage.

But starting on Monday, September 20, 1955, normalcy became a thing of the past as the family plunged headlong into Vermont's own version of The Twilight Zone.

On that day one of the daughters noticed a quantity of water had collected in the concave seat of a wooden chair in her bedroom. As she was about to clean it up, she noticed a second puddle on the floor. Where had it come from? Nothing had spilled. Nothing was leaking. It wasn't raining outside and no water pipes ran through her room.

Almost immediately other family members began noticing pools of water here and there on the first and second floors of the house.

What started as a trickle quickly became a downpour. Over the first two days the family collected 13 pails of water. But no one could determine where it was coming from—it just seemed to appear.

This water from nowhere saturated the contents of their bureau drawers and soaked the clothing in their closets. Dishes, cups, and glasses filled with water. Continual mopping and sponging did no good; it was like trying to bail out a sinking ship.

Mattresses, pillows, and living room furniture got so wet they had to be removed from the house.

The baffled MD called in friends and neighbors hoping someone could make sense this unique water problem. The puzzled Windsorites looked around, scratched their heads, shrugged and observed that the air didn't seem to be unusually damp. Or warm. Or cold. They didn't notice any mist or haze. And—try as they might—they could discern no possible source for the accumulating water.

Yet water continued to appear. In drawers. Bowls. Dishes. On chairs and all over the floor. The Claremont [NH] *Daily Eagle* reported that on occasion it actually rained inside the house.

DAILY E[illegible]

SERVING CLAREMONT AND THE T[illegible]

VOL. XLI, NO. 234 Claremont, New Hampshire, Thursday, October 6, 1955

Windsor Family Forced to Leave As Water from Nowhere Moves In

WINDSOR MYSTERY is occurring in this Cherry street residence owned by Dr. and Mrs. William Waterman. Their family has been forced to vacate the house due to a moisture problem. They are now living in a trailer while their clothes and personal belongings dry in the garage at left. Daily Eagle Photo—[illegible]

By Ken Roberts

WINDSOR Oct. 5—Dr. and Mrs. William M. Waterman have been driven from their Cherry street home by water.

Origin of the water has not, as yet, been determined. But its presence forced them last Sunday to evacuate their home—a two-story, seven-room, wooden-frame, shingled-exterior, brown-and-white house. The couple, with their two daughters, now occupy a trailer which they have placed in their front yard.

[illegible] the house. Water would appear on the floor, on tables, in or on anything except walls and ceilings.

More would come in the evening than at any other time of day, but it was almost constantly noticeable somewhere in the house.

Why it came and whence it came remains a mystery. Electricians, contractors, plumbers, insulating concerns, furnace agents—none of these have offered any satisfactory theories.

[illegible] viously. Furthermore, none of their neighbors has reported similar difficulties.

The solution, observers believe, must be somewhere in the air within the confines of the Waterman home. But no answer has as yet been found.

The house is situated approximately 200 yards from Kennedy pond, which of late has been engulfed by heavy fog and mist during the morning and at night. But this condition, Dr. Waterman [illegible] is not unusual.

The doctor described one instance when he was carrying a bowl of grapes from the kitchen. By the time he got to the living room, the bowl had filled with water almost in front of his eyes.

The family summoned various experts hoping to get to the bottom of things: plumbers, electricians, insulation installers, furnace specialists—even a dowser, but no one could offer a realistic explanation.

However, the perplexed experts were able to make a few interesting observations: there were no broken water lines or sweating pipes; there was no problem with ground water or seepage from a well or spring. Perhaps odder still, the walls and ceilings were not afflicted. They, and the insulation inside the walls, remained perfectly dry. And—perhaps most remarkable for a Vermont house—there was no water in the basement.

Sometimes, when things seemed to be drying out, the family would leave for a while only to return to a house that appeared to have been flooded.

So where was the water coming from?

How could it just appear before their eyes?

And why now, after living in the house for nine years with no similar problems?

The doctor said, "To...stand in the middle of a room, feeling no dampness, and to watch the water mount on the boards about you, is an experience almost terrifying!"

Things climaxed during the first weekend in October.

Water cascaded from the kitchen cupboards, streamed from under the electric stove, and dripped from the living room piano. The family had finally had enough. They had already moved what furniture they wanted to save into the garage; now they too moved out, driven from their home by the fantastic flood.

All four moved into a trailer in their front yard. Where—it may be important to note—the phenomenon did not follow.

When the Associated Press picked up the story, newspapers from all around the world began phoning to get more information. Letters with questions, explanations and prayers arrived almost every day. Endless lines of curiosity seekers paraded by the house on foot and in cars. Numerous eccentrics imposed themselves into the situation with scenarios involving divine or demonic intervention.

Then, about a month after the phenomenon started, it stopped. The end, like the beginning, came without explanation. In hopes of cutting off the flow of curiosity seekers, the doctor issued a press release saying the problem had been solved. But it hadn't been solved—it just stopped.

Over the weekend of October 22 and 23 the family began moving back into their house. And, as life returned to something resembling normal, the high strangeness in Windsor slipped little by little from memory.

Today, whenever I reflect on this strange tale, I can almost believe there really is some sort of cosmic joker who enjoys involving unsuspecting souls in outlandish antics such as these.

And if the unsettling events at Windsor were a cosmic joke, I should close by telling you the punchline.

You may have noticed that so far I haven't mentioned the name of the unfortunate family. Believe it or not, their name was...Waterman.

AUTHOR'S NOTE: Odd that I could grow up in Windsor County, so close to where this happened, and never hear about it. Then again, I was a wee lad in 1955; we didn't have a TV, and I wasn't in the habit of reading newspapers.

I discovered it when I was adult, well into my explorations into weirdness. The thing is, the place I read about it, *Unexplained Mysteries of the 20th Century* by Janet and Colin Bord (1989), kind of tossed it off, as if it were no big deal.

In fact, they only devoted 45 words to it, and those words were: "A similar case was reported from, Vermont (USA), in September 1955 when the Waterman family found beads of moisture on their furniture which returned however frequently it was removed. A shallow dish being carried from one room to another filled with water on the way."

That's it! Just 45 words in a book of over 400 pages!

Needless to say, it caught my attention. Especially because

no one had picked up on the odd synchronicity of water and the name "Waterman". An odd phenomenon in and of itself.

I decided to follow up on it as something that might be mildly interesting. (As you have seen, "mildly" turned out to be the wrong adjective.)

Sometime around 1992 I began recording commentaries in Windsor, where Vermont Public Radio was headquartered at the time. While in town I decided to take the opportunity to see what I could see. My first stop was the Windsor Public Library. The young librarian wasn't a local and had no recollection of the incident. But she kindly put me in touch with a long-time member of the library's board of directors.

I felt a bit awkward asking this dignified community member what might be a conversation-ending question. I don't remember the exact words, but the conversation went something like this:

"Do you remember a Dr. Waterman?"

"Oh why sure, 'course I do. He helped get us the hospital..."

"And he lived right here in town?"

"Hmmm-hmmm. His house is up on Cherry Street."

"Yes, that's the place. Now, do you recall anything unusual happening there back in 1955? Something involving water...?"

A long, thoughtful pause, and then... yes, she did remember!

Not only did she recall the incident, but she was still corresponding with one of Dr. Waterman's daughters, who, as it turned out, lived in the next town over from me. She even gave me the daughter's phone number.

Rarely do things fall this perfectly into place.

It took me a while to work up the courage to call her. These inquiries often do not go well. One takes the chance of reopening old wounds, stirring up unpleasant memories, or at the very least, embarrassing the interviewee.

After a certain period of trepidation, I finally phoned her. I remember she kind of laughed and said, "Jeez, I'm surprised anyone remembers that!"

Ice broken, we had a pleasant and informative chat. She verified everything, and even mailed me a bunch of newspaper clippings about the strange event.

Via my books and radio commentary series I brought the Waterman Mystery once more to the public's attention.

As it turned out, a lot of people remembered the incident. While being interviewed on a call-in radio show we heard from a neighbor of Dr. Waterman's who had been mystified by the events as they unfolded and had feared they would begin at her house nearby. They didn't.

I also heard from the son of the plumber who was the first professional on the scene to try to solve the problem. He couldn't. His son said, "My father was puzzled for the rest of his life about the way water behaved in that house."

In the many years that have passed, no true solution has been forthcoming. When people ask me if I truly believe weird things happen in this world, I often cite this case. Beyond a doubt, it happened. Exactly what happened is as big as mystery now as it was in 1955.

THOSE ENIGMATIC EDDYS

Here in Vermont, in the 1870s, the little mountain town of Chittenden became known as "The Spirit Capital"—not of Vermont. Not of America. Not of the world!—But "The Spirit Capital of the Universe."

I guess that's because visitors included people from this sphere, but also many others.

It was there in a remote and ramshackle farmhouse that the mysterious Eddy brothers—William and Horatio—conducted a series of seances during which they produced virtually all of the Spirit manifestations known at the time, including rapping from nowhere, objects moving by themselves, mystical healing, human levitation, remote vision, and more.

There, in the presence of multiple witnesses, legions of phantoms danced to music played by invisible musicians.

But what earned the brothers worldwide attention was the full physical materializations of recognizable dead people.

These materializations won the brothers their reputation as mediums and won the town of Chittenden its unique title. Everyone who attended the seances saw the phantoms. Some spectators recognized long-deceased friends and relatives.

It is well-documented that people traveled from far and wide to witness these phenomena. Some thought they were seeing miracles. An equal number suspected trickery. So—in 1874—the events at the Eddy farmhouse became the subject of Vermont's first official case of ghostbusting.

Col. Henry Steel Olcott was assigned by the *New York Daily Graphic* to visit Chittenden. The newspaper instructed him to determine whether the Eddy brothers were villains or visionaries. If they were gifted spirit mediums, he'd say so. If they were ingenious charlatans he'd expose them and let public contempt do its worst.

In either event, Col. Olcott was determined to be fair.

The Eddys, he learned, claimed they were descended from a long line of psychics dating back to the 1692 Salem witch trials where a maternal ancestor had been convicted. Their mother supposedly had various psychic gifts, but their father—convinced her powers came from the Devil—forced her to conceal them.

But unseen forces followed the Eddy boys from the cradle to their brief attempt at education.

Invisible entities disrupted the one-room schoolhouse, pounding walls, hurling objects through the air. Mr. Eddy beat his sons, yet the strange antics continued.

Then, perhaps in a moment of inspiration, he realized he could put his sons on exhibition and make some money. For a tidy sum he released them to a traveling showman who toured them throughout the U.S., Canada, and Europe.

Their performances withstood the most thorough and the

most brutal "psychic investigators," but left them scarred. When their parents died, William and Horatio returned home, bearing the wounds of ropes, hot coals, even bullets.

By the time Col. Olcott met them they'd become cold, suspicious and unfriendly, but in the three months he spent with them, he witnessed wildly fantastic displays of spiritual phenomena every night... except Sundays.

For the most part, the seances worked like this. Each night at seven o'clock guests and visitors assembled on wooden benches before a dimly lighted platform in their 17 by 37 foot séance room. William Eddy, the primary medium, would mount the platform. He'd say, "I am ready," then he'd enter a tiny closet known as his "spirit cabinet." Silence followed. Then far-off voices spoke. Music played. Tambourines came to life, soared around the stage. Hands appeared, grappling, waving, touching the spectators.

Ethereal forms began to emerge from the cabinet. One at a time. In groups. Twenty, even thirty in the course of an evening. Some were completely visible, seemingly solid—others were partially materialized or transparent. They varied in size from that of an infant, to well over six feet (William himself was only 5'9").

Although the majority of ghostly visitors were elderly Vermonters or American Indians, a vast array of nationalities appeared in costume: black Africans, Kurds, Russians, Asians, and more.

One woman conversed in Russian with the specter of her dead husband.

Col. Olcott was well versed in the methods of stage magicians and fraudulent mediums. His detailed examinations exposed no trickery with the spirit cabinet. What's more, he concluded that such a show would require a whole troupe of actors and several trunks full of costumes. With the help of carpenters and engineers, Col. Olcott proved there was simply no place to hide people and props.

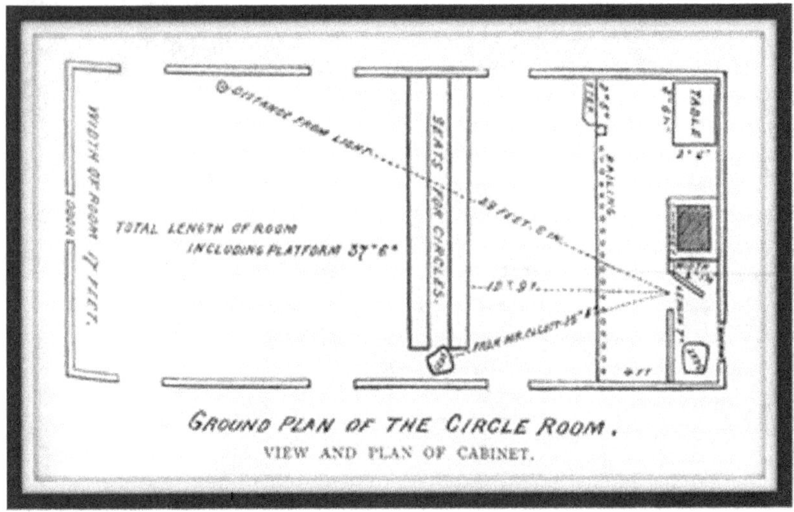

The Colonel remained at the farmhouse for ten weeks. Despite his dislike the gloomy brothers, he became absolutely confident of their otherworldly powers.

In addition to his newspaper articles, he chronicled his experience in a remarkable book called *People From the Other World.*

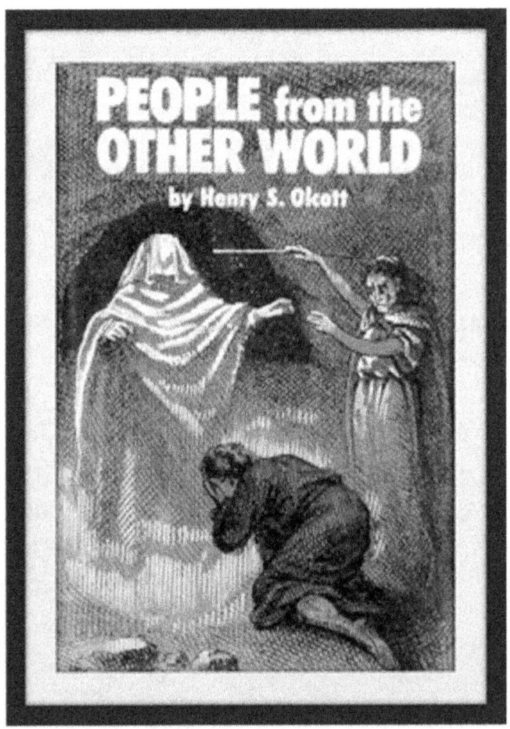

His documentation is full of detailed drawings of the house and its construction. He also reproduces statements from respectable carpenters and tradespeople who examined everything for trickery. When he found none, he proclaimed the phenomena genuine and he came away a changed man.

SECTIONAL VIEW OF CABINET.

So what are we to make of all this today? Were the Eddy phenomena real?

More than a century after the fact, it's impossible to say. Admittedly, we're tempted to dismiss the events of Spiritualism, to say that in a simpler, less sophisticated era investigators were... simpler and less sophisticated.

Surely we would never be so easily duped.

Maybe so, maybe not. But in my opinion, something grand and mysterious happened in Chittenden in the 19th century. Exactly what remains a puzzle. Did the Eddy brothers actually communicate with the dead?

Who can say?

As with all things supernatural, it all comes down to a matter of faith.

Spiritualism's popularity faded in the first quarter of the 20th century. Hundreds of fraudulent mediums were exposed, and investigators like Harry Houdini made it a crusade to defame every single one of them.

Stage magicians incorporated "Spirit Shows" into their magic acts and, after a pretty successful run, the American Spiritualism that might have elevated mankind to a loftier stage of spiritual evolution, was relegated to the domains of entertainment, charlatanism, and delusion.

The Eddy brothers lived on in Chittenden until Horatio died 1922. When William followed ten years later—at age 99—he took the solution to Vermont's strangest mystery with him to the grave.

Since then—as far as we know—he's held his silence.

AUTHOR'S NOTE: There is so much more to say about the Eddy's. I have studied their story for years. To me it's Vermont's strangest tale... not to mention our most colorful and enduring mystery.

What in the world happened there?

Some years ago *Vermont Life* magazine asked me to do an article about the brothers ("Beyond Belief", Autumn, 1999). The assignment was to try to debunk them. I made a sincere effort. I figured if I could solve the problem, I would then have a good mystery yarn instead of a good supernatural tale. Either way I'd come out of it with a wonderful story.

I put a lot of hours into that article. I poured over long out-of-print books and newspapers, I spoke with many residents of Chittenden and Brandon, I even interviewed one elderly man, Ed Davenport, who had actually known the Eddys.

> Among those that I saw were a number of my own friends—one my old friend Mr C. Redding, who lived at Inglewood and Dunedin. He was killed about four years ago at the central shaft of the Hoosac Tunnel. He appeared twice—walked from the cabinet on the platform, dressed precisely as he was when last I saw him. He could not speak, but answered my questions by raps with his hand. I also saw my sister and brother, who passed away over twenty-six years ago; also, a cousin, who passed on a few years since; also, a young girl who lived near us. Honto, an Indian girl, appeared a good many times. She played on the organ, and sang and danced. One evening, she invited two ladies and two gentleman to dance with her. They danced about ten minutes. Honto remained out so long that she had no power to get back into the cabinet, but faded away on the stage.

Doing my best Sherlock Holmes, I was able to impeach the Eddys to some degree, but I was not able to disprove the most spectacular of their wonders. I found myself in a situation similar to Col. Olcott's, back in 1875. He spent ten weeks with the brothers looking for trickery. When he found none, he had no choice but to conclude that the phenomena were genuine.

Just as he outlined his investigative efforts in his book *People from the Other World*, I outlined mine in my *Vermont Life* article. Then I expanded on the details in my book *Vermont's Haunts* [2011].

So what should we conclude about the enigmatic Eddys?

In the end it all comes down to the investigator, Col. Olcott. Was he a reliable witness? Did he report accurately and without bias? Certainly his training and intellect were up to the task. He was clearly a high achiever with a logical scientific mind—a hybrid of scientist, investigator, reporter, and attorney. It is unlikely he was deceived, unless, of course, he deceived himself.

One thinks of Sir Authur Conan Doyle, the medical man turned writer who created the coldly logical and impossible-to-deceive Sherlock Holmes. The question is often asked, How could the father of Sherlock Holmes turn around and fanatically embrace Spiritualism?

Col. Olcott's conversion seems somewhat analogous.

The course of his life changed drastically after his visit to Chittenden. It was there he met Madame Helena Petrovna Blavatsky, a Spiritualist, world traveler, and mystic. Together they went on to establish the Theosophical Society, which is a whole story in and of itself.

On May 25, 1880, Col. Olcott publicly converted to Buddhism. It is likely he was the first native born American to do so. While almost forgotten in America, he is revered in India and Sri Lanka for his efforts revitalizing Buddhism.

His fascinating life story is complex and difficult to integrate with any sort of precision into the events at the Eddy homestead. For literary convenience I have repeatedly relegated the colonel to a mere character in the Eddy drama. In truth, he is worthy of a story all his own, but, alas, I fear I will not be the one to write it.

For more information on Col. Olcott, see his autobiographical work *Old Diary Leaves* and also Stephen Prothero's biography of Col. Olcott, *The White Buddhist: The Asian Odyssey of Henry Steel Olcott.*

Joe Citro recording the audio book !

A WARNING TO THE CURIOUS

Seeing is not always believing. As you've probably already guessed, I have doctored a lot of the pictures in this book. If you see specters lurking around bridges and buildings, it was just me messing with photo manipulating tools. Though the pictures may be doctored, the locations are real (except maybe the picture of hell).

With that confession out of the way, I'd like to say a few words of thanks to those who helped me turn these scripts into a book.

Chris Albertine for helping me edit the original scripts and for the photo of me in the recording studio.

Susan R. Shepherd gave me a lot of help with some of the research, especially with the story about Champ on land.

Scott Mardis, who is the local expert on Champ, has kept me up-to-date.

Steve Bissette allowed me to use several of his wonderful illustrations, including one of the Lake Champlain Monster and two pictures of endangered cows.

A special thank you to Buzz Fisher, who went out of his way to get me the photographs of what we may presume to be John P. Weeks's final resting place. Check out some of Buzz's other great work at CreativeOutbursts.com.

Most of the photographs are my own, although some are from my collection and various other ancient sources. It should be obvious which is which.

THE END
(of the book)

ABOUT THE AUTHOR

Joseph A. Citro (on right) is an expert in New England weirdness. In over a dozen publications—novels and nonfiction—he has guided readers through a dark, disturbing, and often sinister landscape traditionally portrayed with sunny skies above quaint villages. His nonfiction books include *Passing Strange, Cursed in New England,* and many more. Additionally, Mr. Citro has authored five acclaimed novels, among them *Shadow Child, Lake Monsters, Deus-X: The Reality Conspiracy* and a collection of short fiction called *Not Yet Dead.* You can reach him on Facebook or via the electronic Ouija board at . . .

BLOG: http://josephacitro.blogspot.com

WEB: http://www.josephacitro.com

CROSSROAD
PRESS

CPSIA information can be obtained
at www.ICGtesting.com
Printed in the USA
BVHW07s0955110618
518745BV00015BA/201/P